Dear Parent:
Your child's love of reading starts here!

Every child learns to read in a different way and at his or her own speed. You can help your young reader improve and become more confident by encouraging his or her own interests and abilities. You can also guide your child's spiritual development by reading stories with biblical values and Bible stories, like I Can Read! books published by Zonderkidz. From books your child reads with you to the first books he or she reads alone, there are I Can Read! books for every stage of reading:

 SHARED READING
Basic language, word repetition, and whimsical illustrations, ideal for sharing with your emergent reader.

 BEGINNING READING
Short sentences, familiar words, and simple concepts for children eager to read on their own.

 READING WITH HELP
Engaging stories, longer sentences, and language play for developing readers.

 READING ALONE
Complex plots, challenging vocabulary, and high-interest topics for the independent reader.

 ADVANCED READING
Short paragraphs, chapters, and exciting themes for the perfect bridge to chapter books.

I Can Read! books have introduced children to the joy of reading since 1957. Featuring award-winning authors and illustrators and a fabulous cast of beloved characters, I Can Read! books set the standard for beginning readers.

A lifetime of discovery begins with the magical words "I Can Read!"

Visit www.icanread.com for information on enriching your child's reading experience.
Visit www.zonderkidz.com for more Zonderkidz I Can Read! titles.

Don't neglect to do good. Don't forget to
share with others. God is pleased with
those kinds of offerings.
— Hebrews 13:16 NIrV

ZONDERKIDZ

All Is Fair When We Share
©2013 Big Idea Entertainment, LLC. VEGGIETALES®, character names, likenesses and
other indicia are trademarks of and copyrighted by Big Idea Entertainment, LLC.
All rights reserved.
Illustrations ©2011 by Big Idea Entertainment, LLC.

This title is also available as a Zondervan ebook.
Visit www.zondervan/ebooks.

Requests for information should be addressed to:

Zonderkidz, 3900 *Sparks Drive, Grand Rapids, Michigan* 49546

Library of Congress Cataloging-in-Publication Data
Poth, Karen.
     All is fair when we share / Karen Poth.
       pages cm. — (I can read) (Zonderkidz veggietales)
     ISBN 978-0-310-74169-5 (softcover)
     I. VeggieTales (Television program) II. Title.
  PZ7.P83975All 2014
  [E] —dc23   2013034797

Scripture quotations marked NIrV unless otherwise indicated, are taken from The
Holy Bible, *New International Reader's Version®, NIrV®.* Copyright © 1995, 1996, 1998 by
Biblica, Inc.™ Used by permission. All rights reserved worldwide.

Any Internet addresses (websites, blogs, etc.) and telephone numbers in this book are
offered as a resource. They are not intended in any way to be or imply an endorsement
by Zondervan, nor does Zondervan vouch for the content of these sites and numbers
for the life of this book.

All rights reserved. No part of this publication may be reproduced, stored in a retrieval
system, or transmitted in any form or by any means—electronic, mechanical, photocopy,
recording, or any other—except for brief quotations in printed reviews, without the
prior permission of the publisher.

Zonderkidz is a trademark of Zondervan.

Editor: Mary Hassinger
Art direction: Karen Poth
Cover design: Karen Poth
Interior design: Ron Eddy

Printed in China

14 15 16 17 18 19 /DSC/ 13 12 11 10 9 8 7 6 5 4 3 2

All Is Fair When We Share

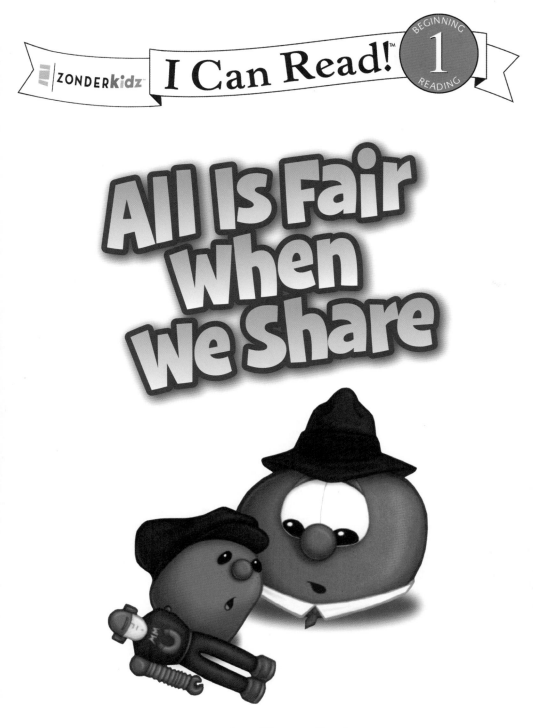

story by Karen Poth

My name is Detective Larry.

This is Detective Bob.

Bob carries a badge.

I carry my badger.

Together we solve mysteries.

Here is one of our stories.

Bob and I were in the car.

RING!

A call came in.

It was Percy Pea.

We drove to his house.

When we got there,
Percy was in his room.
He looked mad.

"My Mighty Man toy is missing,"
Percy said.

"My little brother took it."

This was not good.
Bob and I had to
think fast!

We took Percy to our office.
We looked at a line-up
of Mighty Man toys.

"Are any of these yours?" Bob asked.

"No," Percy said.
"My Mighty Man
has one arm."

"Why?" I asked.

"Lil' Pea broke it," Percy said.

"That's why he can't play with my toys."

Percy left
the station.

"This is hard," Bob said.
"Percy should share
with his brother."

We went back
to Percy's house.
Mom Pea answered
the door.

"Percy and Lil' Pea

fight all the time," she said.

"They won't share anything."

We went up to the boys' room.

It was not good.

There was a line of tape
in the middle of the room.
"Stay on your side," Percy told Lil' Pea.

"He thinks I took his toy,"

Lil' Pea said.

"But I didn't do it."

"Did you BREAK the toy?" Bob asked.

"No," said Lil' Pea.

"Percy broke it when he
took it from me."

"Is this true?" Bob asked Percy.

"Well, yes," Percy said.

"But he shouldn't have had

my Mighty Man."

"You mean THIS Mighty Man?"
Lil' Pea said.

He was holding Percy's toy.

It was covered with dust.

"Where was it?" Percy asked.

"Under the dresser," said Lil' Pea.

"It must have fallen."

Bob said, "When you don't share,
everything gets broken.
Even friendships."

Percy was quiet.

But I wasn't.

I was sad.

I wanted the boys
to be friends again.

"I'm sorry," Percy said
to Lil' Pea.
"I should have shared."
"That's okay," Lil' Pea said.

Percy took the
tape off the floor.

Bob and I left the Pea house.

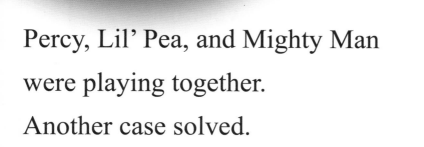

Percy, Lil' Pea, and Mighty Man
were playing together.
Another case solved.

"I'll share my badger
with you," I told Bob,
"if you'll share your badge."